Stand Up for Caring
Growing Character

By Frank Murphy

21st Century
Junior Library

CHERRY LAKE
Publishing

Published in the United States of America by
Cherry Lake Publishing
Ann Arbor, Michigan
www.cherrylakepublishing.com

Reading Adviser: Marla Conn, MS, Ed., Literacy specialist, Read-Ability, Inc.

Photo Credits: ©A3pfamily/Shutterstock, cover, 1; ©LightField Studios/Shutterstock, 4; ©Monkey Business Images/Shutterstock, 6; ©PAKULA PIOTR/Shutterstock, 8; ©fizkes/Shutterstock, 10; ©Monkey Business Images/Shutterstock, 12; ©Karen Grigoryan/Shutterstock, 14; ©Africa Studio/Shutterstock, 16; ©YAKOBCHUK VIACHESLAV/Shutterstock, 18; ©MNStudio/Shutterstock, 20

Library of Congress Cataloging-in-Publication Data

Names: Murphy, Frank, 1966- author.
Title: Stand up for caring / written by Frank Murphy.
Description: Ann Arbor : Cherry Lake Publishing, 2019. | Series: Growing
    character | Includes bibliographical references and index.
Identifiers: LCCN 2019007376| ISBN 9781534147409 (hardcover) | ISBN
    9781534148833 (pdf) | ISBN 9781534150263 (pbk.) | ISBN 9781534151697
    (hosted ebook)
Subjects: LCSH: Caring—Juvenile literature.
Classification: LCC BJ1475 .M88 2019 | DDC 177/.7—dc23
LC record available at https://lccn.loc.gov/2019007376

Cherry Lake Publishing would like to acknowledge the work of The Partnership for 21st Century Skills. Please visit *www.p21.org* for more information.

Printed in the United States of America
Corporate Graphics

CONTENTS

Your family and friends show they care by helping you
when you need them.

What Is Caring?

Layla sighed. "I can't do this!" she said as she erased another incorrect answer.

"Math homework?" asked her dad.

"Yup. It's **frustrating**!"

"How can I help?" asked her dad as he sat down next to her.

Layla felt calmer. She knew her dad would be **patient** and guide her to better understand her homework.

It is easy to make friends when you are a caring person.

Layla's dad cares about Layla and her learning. When you are caring, you look for what other people need. Then you do something to help. It might be simply saying something nice to **encourage** someone. It might be taking action and doing something to help someone.

Think!

Think about a time when someone showed you that they care about you. How did their actions make you feel? Consider writing them a thank-you letter, no matter how long ago it happened.

Listening to someone when they ask you for help is a way
to show that you care.

Being a Caring Person

There are many ways to show that you care at home. Layla likes spending time with her cousin Mikaela, who lives with her. She helps Mikaela when she is having problems with friends.

A young person can also be caring toward adults. Layla always listens to her parents when they talk to her. She does the chores her parents ask her to do.

Always say "thank you" when someone gives you a gift.

A caring person tries not to say or do mean, selfish, or hurtful things. They think before they say or do something. And they think about how what they say or do will **affect** someone.

Once, Layla's grandmother bought her a new sweatshirt. Layla didn't like the sweatshirt very much. But she didn't want to hurt her grandmother's feelings. Layla showed she was caring by thanking her grandmother and wearing the sweatshirt anyway.

Being kind to new students at school shows that you are a caring and thoughtful person.

There are ways you can be caring at school. Mikaela made friends with a new student and sat with her at lunch. Each night, Layla brought homework assignments to a sick classmate who missed a week of school. Caring people like Layla and Mikaela don't bully or tease others. They even stood up to a group of girls who were being mean to a younger student.

Create!

Talk with your family about caring. Make a list of kind things you can do. Maybe you can write a thank-you letter to a person who does a service, like a firefighter or a soldier. Or tell your mom or teacher you are thankful for their hard work. Keep a journal about how people react to your caring actions.

Helping your neighbors shovel snow is a great way to show you care.

Layla's older brother, Mason, and his friends shovel snow for their neighbors. They always ask the older neighbors first, and they do the work without asking to be paid. The other neighbors offer to pay Mason and his friends to shovel their driveways. Another way they show they care is by doing the best job they can do.

The clothing that doesn't fit you anymore could be a great help to a family in need.

There may be many people in your community who are in need. You can **volunteer** to help. Giving canned foods to a **food pantry** is one way. You could volunteer with a group to help at an **animal shelter** or to wrap presents during holidays.

Look!

Pay attention and you will see people helping others. Keep your eyes and imagination open. You will find many ways to lend a helping hand. If you don't, ask a parent or teacher to help you find ways to help.

Volunteering with a friend doubles the care that you show.
And it's double the fun!

A person can also choose to care for our world. Layla does this by **recycling** paper, bottles, cans, and other materials. Layla and Mikaela work with a group that plants flowers and bushes each spring at a **cemetery**. These provide food and shelter for insects and other animals. The people who visit the cemetery can enjoy the beauty of the plants and flowers.

If you care for other people, they will care for you.

When you are caring, you make other people feel special and important. Acting in a caring way spreads good feelings. Being a caring person is an easy choice. If everyone always did it, the world would be a much better place.

GLOSSARY

affect (uh-FEKT) to change someone or something

animal shelter (AN-uh-muhl SHEL-tur) a place where animals can stay to be safe and protected from danger

cemetery (SEM-ih-ter-ee) a place where dead people are buried

encourage (en-KUR-ij) to give support, confidence, or hope to someone

food pantry (FOOD PAN-tree) an organization that collects gifts of food and then gives the food to people who are hungry and can't afford to buy it

frustrating (FRUHS-trate-ing) making someone feel helpless or uncertain

patient (PAY-shuhnt) able to put up with delays and problems without getting angry

recycling (ree-SYE-kuhl-ing) collecting used items that can be made into new products

volunteer (vah-luh-TEER) offer to do a job for no pay

FIND OUT MORE

BOOKS

Miller, Pat Zietlow. *Be Kind*. New York, NY: Roaring Brook Press, 2018.

Woodson, Jacqueline. *Each Kindness*. New York, NY: Nancy Paulsen Books, 2012.

WEBSITE

Community Service: A Family's Guide to Getting Involved
http://kidshealth.org/parent/positive/family/volunteer.html#
Find out how you and your family can help out in your community.

INDEX

ABOUT THE AUTHOR

Frank Murphy has written several books for young readers. They are about famous people, historical events, and leadership. He was born in California but now lives in Pennsylvania with his family. Frank believes that the best and easiest way to show you care is to be kind in everything that you do.